This igloo book belongs to:

....

igloobooks

Published in 2017
by Igloo Books Ltd
Cottage Farm
Sywell
NN6 0BJ
www.igloobooks.com

Illustrated by Peter Scott
Written by Ronne Randall

Designed by Nicholas Gage

REX001 0317
2 4 6 8 10 9 7 5 3 1
ISBN: 978-1-7867-0530-3

Printed and manufactured in China

A moment like this

igloobooks

I love each day I spend with you. It's such a joy to see how big you are growing. You'll soon be as tall as me. I love to teach you all the things you'll need to know.

Even when you're all grown up,
I'll still love you so.

Sometimes just the two of us have a lazy day.
I love to tell you stories and then you run and play.
We both stretch out together in the afternoon sun.

I love you so much,
my precious little one.

I love it when we splish and splash. The water feels so nice.
For every gentle splash from me, you laugh and splash me twice.
But I don't mind, my little one, because we're having fun.

And we will both be cleaner, when all the splashing's done.

I love it when we cuddle up and keep each other warm.
I'll always keep you safe, through wind, or snow, or storm.
When we huddle close and snuggle up the way we like to do,

I know that nothing will ever change the love I have for you.

When we take a swim, you love it when I float,
slowly through the cool water, like a sailing boat.
I gently kiss your head and then I tickle your tummy.

You just giggle and say,
"I love you, Mommy!"

It's so much fun to play with you. We always laugh a lot.
You wriggle and you giggle, as I find each tickly spot.
Tickly tummy, tickly chin, tickly little nose.

I cover you with lovely tickles,
right down to your toes.

I love those special moments, when you are by my side.
We play and laugh together and I feel such joy and pride.
In the pretty flower meadow, we run wild and free.

I kiss you and I tell you
how much you mean to me.

We have such precious moments, wherever we explore.
We visit special places and we'll soon discover more.
I stay close beside you, to make sure you're not scared.

It really is so wonderful,
when new adventures are shared.

It's lovely when we settle down at the end of the day,
when we've had lots of fun and are tired from all our play.
We snuggle up together and hold each other tight.

I love you and cherish you,
all through the night.

We snuggle up together,
when evening shadows creep.
I softly croon to you, when all the world's asleep.
Whenever you need me, I'll always be there.

You will always be safe,
wrapped in love and care.

I love you, little one.